I0451152

Define Beauty

PRAISE FOR *STORYSHARES*

"One of the brightest innovators and game-changers in the education industry."
– Forbes

"Your success in applying research-validated practices to promote literacy serves as a valuable model for other organizations seeking to create evidence-based literacy programs."

- Library of Congress

"We need powerful social and educational innovation, and Storyshares is breaking new ground. The organization addresses critical problems facing our students and teachers. I am excited about the strategies it brings to the collective work of making sure every student has an equal chance in life."
– Teach For America

"Around the world, this is one of the up-and-coming trailblazers changing the landscape of literacy and education."
- International Literacy Association

"It's the perfect idea. There's really nothing like this. I mean wow, this will be a wonderful experience for young people."   - Andrea Davis Pinkney, Executive Director, Scholastic

"Reading for meaning opens opportunities for a lifetime of learning. Providing emerging readers with engaging texts that are designed to offer both challenges and support for each individual will improve their lives for years to come. Storyshares is a wonderful start."
- David Rose, Co-founder of CAST & UDL

Define Beauty

Bithja Pierre

STORYSHARES

Story Share, Inc.
New York. Boston. Philadelphia

Copyright © 2022 by Bithja Pierre

All rights reserved.

Published in the United States by Story Share, Inc.

The characters and events in this book are fictitious. Any similarity to real persons, living or dead, is entirely coincidental.

Storyshares
Story Share, Inc.
24 N. Bryn Mawr Avenue #340
Bryn Mawr, PA 19010-3304
www.storyshares.org

Inspiring reading with a new kind of book.

Interest Level: Middle School
Grade Level Equivalent: 5.0

9781642614268

Book design by Storyshares

Printed in the United States of America

Storyshares Presents

1

Nine-year-old Alicia Quentin watched her reflection in the mirror. First she met her own gaze. Then her eyes wandered. They settled on one tightly coiled strand of hair. A single drop of water slid down from it until it landed on her towel. Her small brown hand reached up and pulled at the curl. She watched as the hair slowly became longer as she pulled it away from her face.

Alicia was happy at how long her hair had grown. What would it look like if it were straight? She brought the strand of hair closer to her face and pulled it downward to see how long it had grown. But before she could tell, the tight coil slipped from her fingertips and snapped all the way up to her forehead.

Frustration settled inside her. Now she looked at herself in the mirror again, this time seeing her whole head of hair. An annoyed groan came from her throat. As she tried to avert her eyes, her gaze settled on a magazine cover to her left.

The woman on the cover was gorgeous. Alicia was instantly intrigued by the glow of her smooth, fair skin. It seemed so bright—so perfect. The woman's eyes were so blue that they looked as though they'd captured the ocean's depth. The woman's hair was long and shiny. It framed her face in dark, straight lines.

The magazine cover read, "The Most Beautiful Woman in America."

After a long moment, Alicia's gaze went back to her reflection. She watched her dripping hair again, seeing how the water created a gloss around each coiled strand. Suddenly Alicia's eyes burned with tears. Her hair was wrong. So was her skin. And so were her eyes. Everything about her was all wrong.

One small tear left a trail as it slid down Alicia's face. If that woman was the most beautiful woman in America, then Alicia would never be beautiful.

2

"Please line up in an orderly fashion," Mrs. Stanley's voice called out through the gymnasium. Her voice was deep from years of smoking. She stood in the center of the gym and ran a hand through her short, straight hair.

About forty middle schoolers lined up to audition for the musical. Alicia, now thirteen-years-old, watched the line from where she stood. She anxiously twiddled her thumbs. She could do this. She loved singing, after all, and she wasn't bad at acting. Her fellow eighth-graders told her that she was a shoo-in for the lead role. Maybe they were right.

When it was Alicia's turn, Mrs. Stanley smiled at her briefly and handed her a piece of paper. "Hi, sweetie. If you don't know the words, just read the lyrics on this paper." Then Mrs. Stanley stood back to allow Alicia to sing.

As her audition came to an end, Alicia grew more anxious. She returned to the back of the gymnasium. Others standing around her told her how great she'd been. She smiled, feeling her anxiety slowly disappear with their compliments.

Twenty minutes later, auditions ended. Mrs. Stanley returned to the center of the gym and clapped her hands together. "Thank you, everyone, for your incredible auditions! The cast list will be up by Friday."

That Friday took forever to come. But when it finally did, Alicia's nerves had returned. She couldn't wait until school was over. She could hardly focus on anything else for the whole day. When 2:45pm hit, Alicia was one of the first to head to the gym.

She reached the tiny crowd that surrounded the paper, trying to calm her beating heart. She'd be fine, she told herself. Whatever happened, she'd be fine.

But when she saw who had gotten the lead role, she didn't feel fine. She felt inadequate. It was like she was seven years old all over again—and not good enough. Suddenly, Alicia understood why she hadn't gotten the role.

She looked over at the girl who'd gotten the role. It was the girl who couldn't sing very well, and who was too shy to act in front of people. This girl had fair skin and long straight hair. She looked just like the girl in the original movie, from which the musical had been adapted. She also looked just like the woman in the magazine.

Alicia smiled sadly.

"Congratulations," Alicia told the girl.

Her heart sank with every syllable. And two months later when Mrs. Stanley asked Alicia if she would sing for the girl backstage while the girl lip-synched the songs, Alicia's heart sank even further.

Now Alicia knew. That was all she would ever be. She wasn't enough. Someone like her was meant to be in the background. Because just as Mrs. Stanley had later told her, Alicia "didn't quite fit" the role, and she never could.

3

On the first day of junior year, sixteen-year-old Alicia felt at ease. She sat in her father's car on the way to school, her phone in her right hand. Laid-back, Alicia scrolled through her news feed. She smiled at a funny picture and continued on to the next one.

Suddenly, Alicia received a direct message from a friend. When she tapped it, a new image came up on the screen. The image instantly caught Alicia's eye, and she paused to take it in completely. It was a picture of a girl. But this time, the girl didn't have long, straight hair. She didn't have blue eyes that looked like the ocean. No, this time the girl had dark skin and eyes that looked like molten chocolate. Her hair was cut all the way down to her head, and tiny little strands of coiled hair emerged from her scalp. Her smile was so radiant that it glowed brighter than any light Alicia had ever seen.

This, Alicia thought to herself, is the most beautiful woman in America.

Alicia gazed at the picture for a long time, and she found herself thinking back to that day of the audition, nine years ago. That day she'd cried about not being beautiful because she would never look like the woman in the magazine. Now, Alicia couldn't help but think about beauty.

What was beauty, really?

4

Click, click, click.

The sounds from Alicia's footsteps came through the speakers to the entire auditorium. The room was silent as Alicia walked over to the podium. Her graduation gown and cap glimmered under the bright stage lights. She cleared her throat.

"Good morning, faculty, staff, students, and parents. It is my pleasure to be here celebrating the endurance of my senior class, and how far we have come. If there was one word that I would use to describe my class, it would be the word 'beautiful.'"

Alicia looked up from her papers and stared out into the crowd. "Beauty is a concept that many people struggle to define. It is subjective. It differs from person to person. In truth, beauty cannot be described in one simple, concrete way. Despite this fact, I've spent most of my life trying to understand beauty. And after four years with this class, I finally have an understanding.

"Today, I'd like to tell you what it means to be beautiful. When I was seven years old, I looked at magazines and realized I would never look like the women in them. At thirteen, I thought I would never be able to shine like everyone else could. I felt this way because of the color of my skin. I thought that I wasn't beautiful."

A smile slowly formed on Alicia's face. She made eye contact with the members of her class before continuing.

"But then, I learned from everyone sitting in the first few rows. I learned from my fellow classmates that beauty doesn't come from light skin, or long hair, or a perfect body shape. It comes from you. It comes from me. It comes from who we are. And it is magnified by diversity. This class taught me that it is okay to not fit the mold, and not to match the person sitting next to you. My classmates, from you all, I learned that beauty is the world. It is every skin tone, every thought, every argument, every smile, every gender and every mistake.

"I am beautiful, you are beautiful, and there is beauty in everything that we do. This is why I am not worried about my class. I am not worried that we won't become billionaires, or CEOs, or superstars. Everyone shines in a spotlight, each in their own unique way. I have no doubt that we will succeed at everything that we do, as long as we keep the last four years with us. I have grown a lot in the past four years, and I know that each and every member of this class has as well. And if we keep that beauty of this class—of the world—with us, there is nothing that we cannot do."

Alicia took a deep breath, and finished by saying, "To the faculty and parents here today, I thank you for your guidance. And to my classmates, I congratulate you for your success. And to each and every one of you in this auditorium at this moment, you are truly beautiful."

About The Author

Bithja Pierre is a contributing author to the Storyshares library.

About The Publisher

Story Shares is a nonprofit focused on supporting the millions of teens and adults who struggle with reading by creating a new shelf in the library specifically for them. The ever-growing collection features content that is compelling and culturally relevant for teens and adults, yet still readable at a range of lower reading levels.

Story Shares generates content by engaging deeply with writers, bringing together a community to create this new kind of book. With more intriguing and approachable stories to choose from, the teens and adults who have fallen behind are improving their skills and beginning to discover the joy of reading. For more information, visit storyshares.org.

Easy to Read. Hard to Put Down.

Define Beauty

www.ingramcontent.com/pod-product-compliance
Lightning Source LLC
Chambersburg PA
CBHW071231170626
46809CB00005BA/2034